I0782158

GIRL FROM SPACE

Book 1 On a Space Mission

A Contemporary
Story About
the Power of Faith

Written and Illustrated by Nadia Han
Edited by Annie K Preston

Nadia Han was born in Minsk, Belarus. Inspired by working in the Hi-tech business, she decided to leave her hometown and search for opportunities to create her startups in this world. The turnaround in her story took place in China. Now Nadia pursues her career in writing, filmmaking and fashion by visualizing the power of faith. Nadia currently resides with her husband and their two amazing and curious young children in California.

This book and all the adventures are dedicated to **Mister Sure.**

www.GirlFromSpace.com

© 2020 Nadia Han
All rights reserved. This book or any portion thereof may not be reproduced or used in any manner whatsoever without the express written permission of the publisher except for the use of brief quotations in a book review.

This is a work of Space. Names, characters, businesses, places, events, locales, and incidents are the products of Space. Any resemblance to actual persons, living or dead, or actual events is purely space coincidental.
Space stamped.

Second Edition: February 2021
10 9 8 7 6 5 4 3 2 1

Library of Congress Control Number (First Edition): 2020905438

ISBN 978-1-952532-14-6 (hardcover)

CONTENTS

WHITE SPACESHIP

Mister Sure: A beautiful heartbeat overcomes the sound of the universe. The heartbeat belongs to a young slender person with golden hair and long, beautiful legs. Her face has a few freckles and a shiny smile. Her name is Girl From Space.

Girl From Space is on the White Spaceship. She looks out beyond the horizon. Next to her is someone else. It is actually me. My name is Mister Sure. In this book you will join us in all of our adventures! I promise, you will be charged with the only energy of the future - and that is FAITH.

Blue Bag Follow Me: Hey there! I am Blue Bag Follow Me. Hey, wait! I am not just a bag! I am associated with this young person with the peculiar name, Girl From Space. Wait, wait, wait! It is my honor to have such a task. Through me, The Bag, you can see the FAITH. Why through me? I collect her past, her current, and her future using my space magnifier, and I am led by Mister Sure! Well, be patient. Are you ready to connect? HAVE FUN!

Happy Imagination: Cannot wait.

SPACE MAP

Moscow
Minsk
Changchun
Beijing
Shanghai
Damascus
Guangzhou

7

GENESIS

MiNSK
Europe
Poland
BELARUS
Russia
UKRAINE
CHINA

Mister Sure: Girl From Space was born in a quiet place in Eastern Europe called Minsk. Minsk is the capital of the country Belarus.

Blue Bag Follow Me: Let's look together through our space magnifier: the planet Earth - the largest continent Eurasia - then the continent Europe and the region in Europe - Eastern Europe - and then ten million people - Belarus and two million people - Minsk and, finally, there was a family and then a person - Girl From Space. Phew.

Belarus: Ho ho ho. Such an honor!

Minsk: I am actually not a small guy at all. Bye.

Mister Sure: Well, it was not a possible coincidence for this world, but certainly it was possible for me. Right, Blue Bag Follow Me?

Blue Bag Follow Me: Yep.

Mister Sure: Where was I? Okay. Girl From Space was a thin, curious girl. And sometimes, she was a troublemaker.

Blue Bag Follow Me: She was a girl with a happy imagination and a brave heart!

Happy Imagination: Ciao!

Mister Sure: More than anything, Little Girl From Space enjoyed spending summers with her grandparents in a far-away village. She did not need any companions.

There were two major places to explore - the rooftops of old farm buildings and the ancient forest surrounding the village. I will not say anything about the farm animals. She was their close friend, but they were still afraid of her. Haha.

While playing, Girl From Space sang different melodies. Singing helped her to be more courageous, especially while stepping deeper into the ancient forest. And one day Girl From Space was really scared by a big wild bird there!

Brave Heart: Hiccup.

Mister Sure: There was also a huge potato field in the village that seemed endless to Girl From Space. She liked to run through the field and lightly touch the big, healthy-looking, green potato leaves with her palms.

Girl From Space was absolutely free there - playing by herself. As I watched her, I had a forever smile on my face.

Blue Bag Follow Me: Wow, Mister Sure! You already prepared a SPACE MISSION for her!

Mister Sure: Yes. I did.

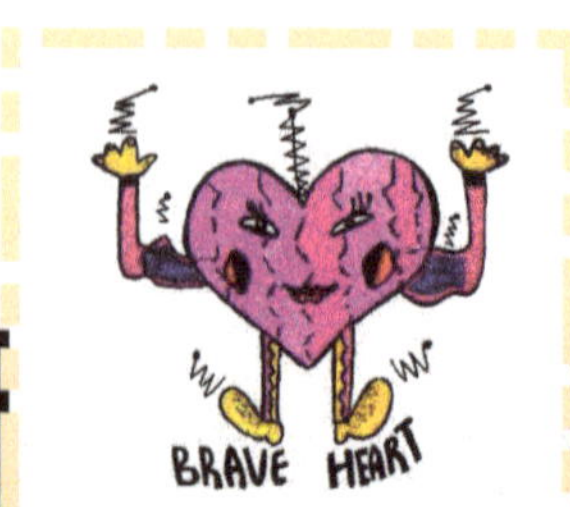

HAPPY
IMACINATION

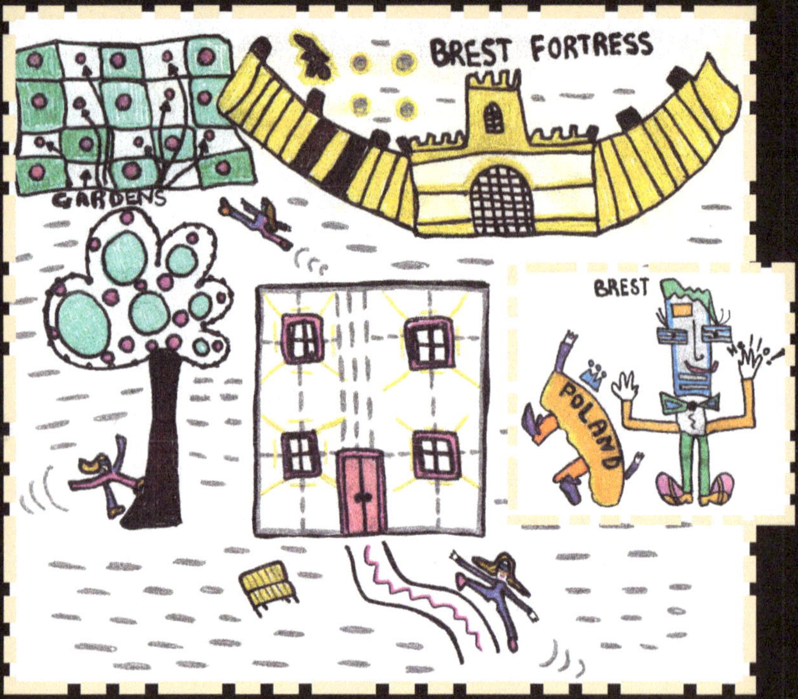

GARDENS
BREST FORTRESS
BREST
POLAND
ME!!!O!!

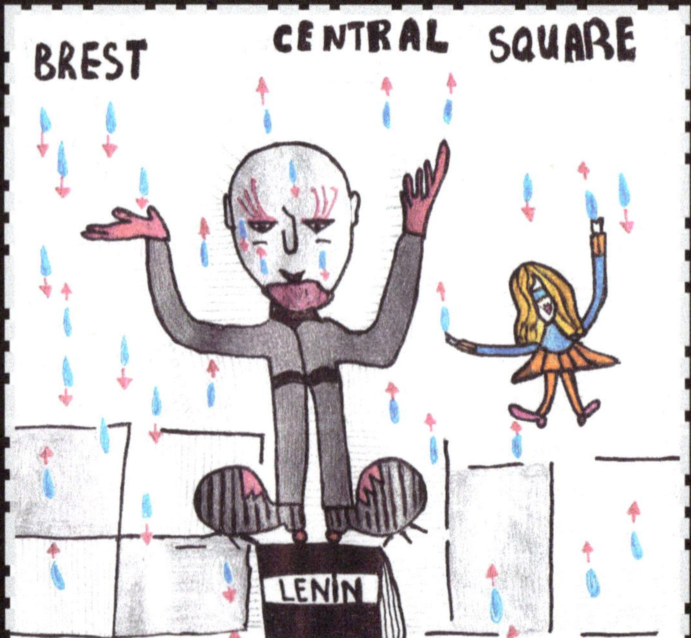

BREST CENTRAL SQUARE
LENIN

But let's keep going.

There was another place Girl From Space liked during her summers in Belarus. It was the town called Brest, on the border with Poland.

Brest: Hello friends, I am famous for my Hero Fortress during the Second World War.

Mister Sure: Girl From Space's relatives owned a garden near that Brest Hero Fortress. They also had a condo in a cute two-story cubic-shaped building built in the 1950s and not far from the main central square. On that central square there was a tall statue of Lenin pointing with his finger. Girl From Space liked to run there during warm heavy rains. It was a wide-open area. And the big drops of rain seemed to shoot into the concrete gray tiles there and immediately jump back up into the air. And she always looked at that big statue with a certain wonder.

Girl From Space: Poor man, he is standing and pointing with his finger somewhere, even during the rain.

Statue Of Lenin: Hey, Little Girl! I am a great Russian revolutionary!

Blue Bag Follow Me: Cuckoo. Girl From Space always surprised everybody with her thoughts and ideas!

Happy Imagination: No kidding.

 So far, the village and Brest were two main destinations for Girl From Space's childhood summers. But her ordinary everyday life was in Minsk. Right, Mister Sure?

Mister Sure: Yes. You are spot on. At the age of seven, Girl From Space was enrolled in a big folk-dance group in Minsk. It was located in a gigantic and gorgeous concert hall with high classical columns. The director of the folk-dance group was a tall Polish Woman wearing a fur hat with a foxtail dangling from the side. She shot loud comments at all of her students during rehearsals. If something went wrong during the concerts, she pierced the children with that stare from her furious eyes behind the stage curtain.

Brave Heart: Hiccup.

 I just found out through our space magnifier that Girl From Space was also performing on Belarus Folk TV!

Mister Sure: Well, I wonder. Blue Bag Follow Me, did you discover that sometimes when she was there, Girl From Space would forget her lines?

Brave Heart: Hiccup.

 Let's see. Yes. That happened! Then she stared at the audience. But if someone else would forget a line - she quickly helped out and filled the gap with her improvisation.

BRAVE HEART

Girl From Space: I am a TV star!

Camera Operators: Here we go.

Blue Bag Follow Me: Girl From Space believed that one day she would become a big television star!

Happy Imagination: It was more than that, Blue Baggie. She believed, at such a young age, that she was a-l-r-e-a-d-y! on a space mission.

Girl From Space: There is something really extraordinary about my future. There is a space mission for me to fulfill. Just thinking about it makes me so JOYFUL.

Mister Sure: Girl From Space had a vision about her space mission. It was very BRIGHT. But let's just keep going.

Here we go!
I am a TV star!

One day when Girl From Space was walking home on the main street of Minsk together with her dancing and singing friends, she heard someone calling her.

American Tourists: Hi, Girl From Space! How are you doing? We are visiting Belarus.

Girl From Space: Hi. I am good. Wow, you are so bright and confident!

Mister Sure: Suddenly, another person interrupted them. That person was pretty famous in Belarus. Her name was easy to remember - Gray Reality Whispering Around.

Gray Reality Whispering Around: I cannot believe my eyes! Get out from my dwelling, guys! And you, Girl From Space, stay away from those people!

Girl From Space: Thank you for your concern, Miss.

Happy Imagination: Blue Baggie, look. Your space magnifier shows that Gray Reality Whispering Around does not have any hair!

Blue Bag Follow Me: Camouflage! Gee whiz, tricksters are persistent!

Mister Sure: Hahaha.

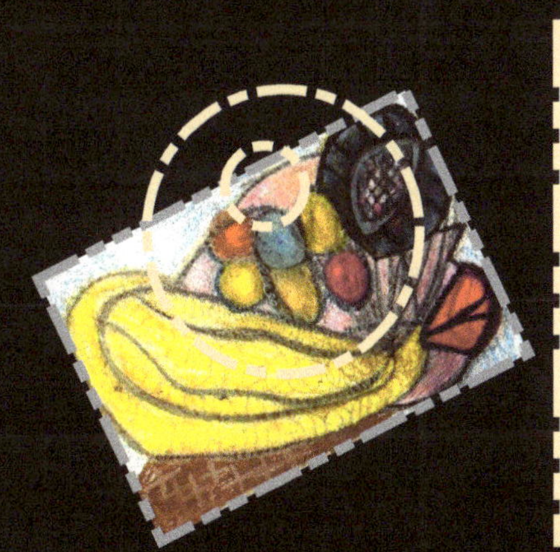

BELARUS
Hohoho

American
Tourists
chewing gum

Let's keep going.

Week by week, year by year, the days slowly passed, and then Girl From Space graduated from school and became a college student.

Professors: We have two simple questions for you, Girl From Space. Are you patriotic enough? What do you already know about the country where you were born?

Belarus: Ho ho ho. Leave her alone. She is a special girl.

 Well, they were kind of right. No?

Mister Sure: Blue Bag Follow Me, do you want to add something here while searching there with your space magnifier?

 Isn't he silly with this pacifier? Oopsy. I mean magnifier.

 I found her, Mister Sure! When Girl From Space was a little girl, she, together with her older sister, used to wait in long lines to buy bread and sour cream using those strange paper tickets, limiting the quantity of food per person.

As she was growing up she saw her grandparents working very hard at the farm, recovering from the damage made by the Communist Party; she saw her relatives in Brest crossing the border to Poland to buy Polish goods and resell them in

Hohoho
BELARUS
PROFESSORS

Super market
Hours: 9-9
Tickets PLEASE!
It is only 8:00AM
Sister
Tickets
Tickets
LOST TICKETS
Tickets
Long Line

Brest on a daily basis. She saw her parents trying to develop their own company and not really being successful with that.

Girl From Space was taught the Belarusian language at school. She also learned about her culture; and about the Chernobyl disaster that happened back in 1986 and polluted most of the country.

She was trying to understand what her purpose was, not only in Belarus, but also on this planet. But she still had a bright, but not clear, vision about it.

Happy Imagination: The last part was amazing. We will work on it.

Professors: We will teach you here to be more patriotic. Get ready. It will be five years of hard and intense work.

Happy Imagination:
Yuck. That sounded just like a verdict in the army. I do not like those professors.

Mister Sure: At that time some revolutionary movements started to rise up in Minsk. Many students would participate in those not-really-safe protests. Always brave and courageous, Girl From Space found herself among the folks on the streets of Minsk, marching with posters and supporting with all her heart as she called out the loud slogan.

Loud Slogan: Freedom to Belarus! Freedom!

CHERNOBYL
1986
DISASTER
BELARUS
FREEDOM

Hohoho
BELARUS

EMPTY JAR
BRAVE HEART

Brave Heart: Hiccup.

Mister Sure: Week by week, year by year, Girl From Space was now very patriotic. But also very disappointed. She gave her beautiful heart for something that was dangerous enough, but not rewarding.

Blue Bag Follow Me: Just like pouring a precious liquid into the jar - little by little, drop by drop, every single day for five years! But what you hoped you had accumulated was all gone and it puzzled you. And then you say to yourself, "How come?" Phew.

Mister Sure: Disappointed Girl From Space felt exactly as you just described: EMPTY.

Space five, Blue Bag Follow Me!

Girl From Space: I do not want to be a revolutionary anymore. I want to reset myself for a much bigger task so I can be filled with my bright vision about my space mission on this planet and maybe in the entire universe.

Happy Imagination: Good-good!

Mister Sure: However, someone was already waiting for Girl From Space.

Gray Reality Whispering Around: It is time to mature. Come on! The true reality in this world is gray reality, it is ME. There are no visions and missions. Trust me!

Blue Bag Follow Me: Gray Reality Whispering Around was trying to enter into Girl From Space's thoughts and STEAL her big bright vision!

Mister Sure: As a result, Girl From Space worked as a small not-deciding-anything manager for one year in a big Russian company in Minsk. Then for another several years she tried to develop her own business, just like her parents did. She felt tired and obviously not important at all.

Did I say at the beginning of the story that miracles were my hobby?

No?

Well, hold on tight here on the White Spaceship! We are making a Hi-tech pit stop.

MAN-RHYTHM

Mister Sure: One day Girl From Space heard a conversation between two women standing at a bus stop. They were talking about a certain *almighty* Man-Rhythm.

Happy Imagination: Almighty? Yum-yum.

Blue Bag Follow Me: Cuckoo. Girl From Space was actually waiting at that bus stop for a bus to take her to the local car market. That day she was ready to buy a new car!

Mister Sure: You both deserve a snack-in-a-tube! Here! Hahaha.

When Girl From Space arrived at the car market, she met a young man there who was eating peanut butter from a jar with a teaspoon, while trying to sell his BMW

SPORTS CAR

sports car. Girl From Space liked his car and the smell of the peanut butter, which was different for her. She decided to buy the car. So, the next morning Girl From Space drove her new sports car to the Hi-tech company of *almighty* Man-Rhythm, who she learned a little more about on the Internet. Girl From Space parked her car and knocked on the door of Man-Rhythm's office.

Man-Rhythm: Hi Dear, I do not think we know each other. Let me take a look at you. Come closer. Are you looking for a job here?

Mister Sure: Girl From Space turned 25 when she started her Hi-tech career working for Man-Rhythm, who was always positive and uplifting.

Happy Imagination: Holy Space. There was no more time for any kind of revolutionary movements.

Man-Rhythm: My Dear Girl From Space, I am introducing you to the most honorable Hi-tech guests around. They are the most Passionate Scientists on this Earth. They are my friends.

Passionate Scientists: Girl From Space, we have so many Hi-tech ideas! Where can we put them?

Girl From Space: Come in! Welcome home! This is the Hi-Tech Park in Minsk!

Mister Sure: Man-Rhythm was happy to arrange the Hi-tech adventures in Moscow, Damascus, Shanghai, and Beijing for Girl From Space.

Man-Rhythm: I dance to the sound of the Hi-tech world. I want Girl From Space to dance together with me!

34

ROLLING

MOSCOW

Mister Sure: The first Hi-tech adventure took Girl From Space to Moscow, a big crowded city in Russia.

Moscow: Hi, Girl From Space! Here, in my huge area, there are tiring hour-long subway rides and lengthy walks. The hotel you are staying in and the food around you are not very good either. Plus, there is no private shower in the room; it is located downstairs and it is a big sauna with no privacy. I am telling you, you will be exhausted! But for sure I have the most intelligent Hi-tech folks that you will enjoy.

Happy Imagination: Huh.

Mister Sure: Someone would surely complain about those not-so-comfortable conditions. But this was just not Girl From Space's style. Instead, she laughed a lot in Moscow, and her colleague shared so many cool and different adventures with Girl From Space; not Hi-tech ones, but simple adventures in her daily life.

Girl From Space: My friend, I am discovering an interesting thing within myself - all these adventures you are telling me are crossing my imagination as one beautiful FILM!

Blue Bag Follow Me: Did her friend say, "Roll it! And… Action!"?

Mister Sure: Hahaha, the White Spaceship shuddered with laughter.

Happy Imagination: It was ME, silly Blue Bag Follow Me.

INNOVATIVE BULBS

Mister Sure: After the so-so exhibition in Moscow, Man-Rhythm launched Girl From Space on her second Hi-tech adventure. This time it was Damascus, a city all the way in Syria.

Damascus: Hi! I am such a fairytale and unique place in the entire world! The one who comes to visit me, never forgets me. Never!

Gray Reality Whispering Around: Never? Really?

Happy Imagination: Incredible. Gray Reality Whispering Around was also there, camouflaging again.

Blue Bag Follow Me: So were we, but safe and comfy on the White Spaceship.

Mister Sure: Attention please. While representing Passionate Scientists during a big exhibit in Damascus, Girl From Space met a very interesting new friend. His name was Innovative Bulbs.

Blue Bag Follow Me: Cuckoo. Innovative Bulbs was the president of the largest electronics company in the world!

Innovative Bulbs: Welcome to my special exhibition of the future! Do you see all those multi-lights in the sky? Girl From Space, our future is so bright. And you are in charge of this future!

41

**Gray Reality
Whispering Around:**
What? What? What?

Mister Sure: During the exhibit, Innovative Bulbs stayed very close to Girl From Space. Every day he was ready to accommodate Girl From Space in whatever she needed.

**Gray Reality
Whispering Around:**
Hey. It does not make any sense what Innovative Bulbs says. You came to Damascus to work and not to dream and drive your imagination about this bright future. What is it? Blah blah blah.

Mister Sure: Girl From Space dove deep, deep, deep into Innovative Bulbs's bright eyes. She was intrigued and felt joyful.

Girl From Space: I cannot ignore what Innovative Bulbs says. Since I was a little child I believed in my space mission.

Blue Bag Follow Me: Was she too naive to believe her childhood vision?

Happy Imagination: This answer is NO on the White Spaceship.

**Gray Reality
Whispering Around:**
Hmm.

DAMASCUS

BLUE PARATROOPER

Mister Sure: We were all still in Damascus. Innovative Bulbs, as we all know, was surrounding Girl From Space during the big Hi-tech exhibit, but outside there was SOMETHING else Girl From Space should know. It was so different in every way there: a dry warm climate, a desert-style landscape and buildings, and the sound of prayers from a big temple that were happening only at certain times of the day.

Girl From Space: I do like walking in this fairytale city, accompanied by this prayer song.

Damascus Market: Hi there. Nice to meet you. I have everything you want, but you are welcome just to walk here and listen to the sounds of my world!

Blue Bag Follow Me: Girl From Space was way too brave. She was walking by herself in a totally different culture. Local people were watching and admiring her courage!

Happy Imagination: That's it! I can see it all clearly n-o-w!

Local Short Tour Man: Hi. I talk greedily with a passionate tongue. Do you want to hear my stories? Here's one. It is about two heroes, Paul and Ananias, that you do not know anything about yet. The story occurred right in the very place where you are standing!

DAMASCUS
MARKET

Tiny Fabric Store: Hey! Come in and check out the glittering cloths I have.

Mister Sure: Girl From Space stepped into the tiny fabric store.

Glittering Cloths On The Walls: Spark, spark.

Mister Sure: Then suddenly, she heard a noise.

Noisy Boots: March, march, march.

Mister Sure: Girl From Space turned around in slow motion of her film and came face-to-face with a very tall and handsome man.

Blue Paratrooper: Hi, Dear Girl From Space. My name is Blue Paratrooper. Believe it or not, I came to you from Space. I have a message for you - in order to succeed in this world, you have to FIRST find freedom. I will call your heart. So please never be worried.

Mister Sure: Blue Paratrooper's eyes radiated a wave of strong free spirit upon Girl From Space. And then he was gone as fast as he appeared.

Noisy Boots: March, march, march.

Echo: Take care! Find freedom first. I will call your heart!

SPARK
SPARK
SPARK
SPARK
SPARK

FREEDOM

Holy-Spaceship-Holy. What was that all about?

Blue Bag Follow Me: It was all about her space mission! Right, Mister Sure?

Mister Sure: Yes, but Girl From Space paused. She did not get it right away. At least it was something for her to think about.

Glittering Cloths On The Walls: Spark, spark.

Mister Sure: Here is an explanation of the space mission. In order to succeed, find freedom first. How do you find freedom? By following your heart. Who is calling your heart? Blue Paratrooper.

Easy? Not really.

Now Girl From Space heard from Blue Paratrooper that word, "freedom." And not only that word. Let's see.

Damascus: Dear Girl From Space, your adventure here is coming to an end. Before you go, have dinner at my favorite place that is high-high up in the mountains. It has an amazing view of the entire ME.

Mister Sure: Girl From Space was sitting at the restaurant and enjoying her dinner and the Damascus night lights, and most importantly she was rolling in her film the image of Blue Paratrooper, his boots, and the glittering cloths' spark-spark.

Girl From Space: Blue Paratrooper said that he came from **Space.**

Mister Sure: Then - and for just one moment - the whole Damascus went dark when it lost electricity. And just like that, the city lit up again!

Was it one of Damascus' favorite ways to say goodbye? Or did Blue Paratrooper cause it? Hahaha.

Let's keep going along on the White Spaceship!

MONKEY AND SHANGHAI

SHANGHAI

Mister Sure: As Girl From Space returned from her adventure in Damascus, there was no time for any thinking about Blue Paratrooper. It was a speedy action film!

Man-Rhythm: There is another place that is waiting for you, Dear. This time we are all going with you. Hurry up!

Mister Sure: It was a big delegation of Passionate Scientists rushing through the airport with their Hi-tech luggage. Girl From Space felt excited. Finally, after a long, long flight, all of them arrived in Shanghai, the fancy city in China.

Shanghai: Salut, Girl From Space! Salut, Man-Rhythm! Salut, Passionate Scientists from Minsk! I am a cosmopolitan city with many futuristic buildings stretching out high up into the sky.

I am ROMANTIC. Oh, I AM. You will fall in love with me. I am the paradise for all of your childhood dreams.

Passionate Scientists: What food shall we order? Everything looks so delicious, Dear.

Girl From Space: Wow. These tasty pink apples in the salad, and the cute little kids walking around, and the sweet romantic autumn foggy air make me feel so romantic, indeed!

Blue Bag Follow Me: Cuckoo. Shanghai was about to win Girl From

Space's heart.

Happy Imagination:
And that was a big thing,
Blue Baggie Follow Me.

Mister Sure: Here is the
fun part.

The very first night, Girl
From Space was sitting
on a big bus, touring
around the best places of
Shanghai. She was in the
very back seat and was
taking in all of the
beautiful buildings and
lights glittering
everywhere she looked,
right into her film. She
was in her own space.

Happy Imagination, you
understand this part
better than anyone else.
Haha.

Suddenly, in a flash Girl
From Space had a vision
of her best and sweetest
childhood dream. It was

about a little monkey in
her room dressed in a
striped pink and black
colored costume, and he
was her pet on a swing.

Blue Bag Follow Me:
Who could even think
about having a real
monkey dressed in a
striped pink-and-black
costume in a room on a
swing?

Happy Imagination: ME!
Silly Blue Baggie on the
White Spaceship.

Mister Sure: Haha. That
was funny.

Now, being happy by
"living" her childhood
dream, Girl From Space
enjoyed every single
moment of the adventure
in the city with her
Passionate Scientists. The
next day when they all
went for a walk after

attending a big Hi-tech exhibition, she tried to bargain at some local stores and she was able to buy a pair of shiny black boots and a wristwatch.

Passionate Scientists: Can you bargain for us too? We all have a list of items to buy for our wives.

Blue Bag Follow Me:
Cuckoo. They all had the same items on their list: a set of silk pillows and pearl necklaces!

Mister Sure: In between the shopping, they tried different foods and just walked and watched all that was surrounding them in Shanghai. Doing this made them feel even happier than the day before. They were all just like little kids again.

There was a moment when everyone in the Hi-tech group was running down the street in the middle of the night under a pour of heavy rain. All of them were laughing and getting really, really wet.

Cabs: Sorry, guys. We are just too busy to help you out.

Girl From Space: But that is okay! I love it this way!

Passionate Scientists: We do, too!

Happy Imagination: Happy-Rain-in-Shanghai... How could they ever leave this city?! I will look for the rainbows in the n-i-g-h-t sky!

TALKING EYES

Mister Sure: After spending two weeks in Shanghai, the happy delegation came home to Minsk. Everyone got back to their routines.

Girl From Space was walking toward her office in the Hi-Tech Park, dressed in her new shiny black boots, when she saw one young man with a funny beard approaching her.

Big Guy: Excuse me, are you Girl From Space?

Girl From Space: Yes.

Big Guy: I heard that you just got back from Shanghai. Looks like you have a nice job and everything is okay in your life. Sorry, I forgot to introduce myself. My name is Big Guy. I am the founder of a newly-created youth community called "RISK." Do you want to join and play a game of opportunities with us sometime?

Blue Bag Follow Me: Cuckoo. It was time for taking some risks.

Happy Imagination: I cannot imagine that word RISK next to you, Baggie.

Mister Sure: It will be time for everyone to take some risks. Let's keep going.

The same day after her work, Girl From Space was on her way to play the game. It was a room with a square table in one of the famous university buildings that was just across the street from her office. There were three students sitting at the table in the room. Girl From Space waved at each of them and sat on the one available chair left at the table.

Big Guy greeted everyone and started the game. He was holding the cards with opportunities written on them. During the game the players were taking their turns to proceed with their own choices, while facing the opportunities Big Guy was announcing for them from the cards.

Blue Bag Follow Me: It was fun to play that game. It was all about choices!

Happy Imagination: Do we have that special drum here on the White Spaceship? Hey, brilliant Blue Bag Follow Me, pass me one, please.

Blue Bag Follow Me: Here.

Happy Imagination: Tom-tom. Tom-tom-tom. To risk or to skip risking? Tom-tom. Tom-tom-tom. And skip it again? Tom-tom-tom. Or to risk, risk again and keep on risking. Tom-tom-tom-tom-tom-tom-t-o-o-o-o-o-o-m!

Mister Sure: Hahaha. That was very special! Girl From Space quickly figured out the game and the opportunities, and she learned about Big Guy, too.

Girl From Space: Players are losing chances to win because those chances are usually so tiny to discover, they do not

sound like a chance at all. But then, when you do something DIFFERENT, you actually enter a narrow gate into another reality!

Mister Sure: Soon Girl From Space was able to beat all of the players, who, by the way, were all guys. And the next night, and the other next night and the other one after that, Girl From Space showed up to play the game. She looked elegant and smart, and she stared at Big Guy with a smile of wonder.

Girl From Space: There is something special about Big Guy and his eyes, shining straight on me.

Eyes: Hey! Girl From Space! Awake?

Girl From Space: Awake? I think I understand what he means.

Mister Sure: Even Girl From Space still could not process Blue Paratrooper's message about the freedom; instead, her mind penetrated with ideas about another possible REALITY in this world. She was halfway to understanding her space mission.

How is everyone doing on the White Spaceship? Who wants another snack-in-a-tube?

Blue Bag Follow Me: Oh, yum! I would gladly enjoy another snack!

STARTUPS

Hi-Tech
ART
COLLABORATION
SPORT
FASHION
Cool!
Hi-Tech
IT
HAPPY IMAGINATION

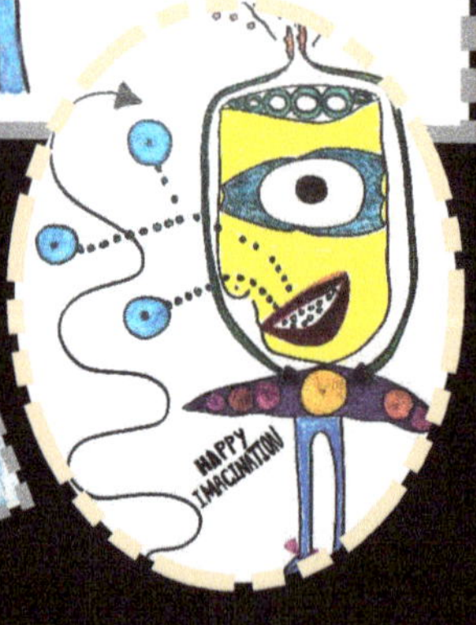

Mister Sure: Man-Rhythm noticed that after all of her Hi-tech adventures, Girl From Space became bolder and more confident. He was also happy about how she was completing her tasks at work. She worked harder.

Man-Rhythm: Look at you! You are such a successful Hi-tech girl! Do you want to get more serious into the Hi-tech world and study venture capital?

Blue Bag Follow Me: Girl From Space liked to "venture" since her childhood!

Happy Imagination: I do not think you would survive without ME there on Earth, Silly Baggie Follow Me.

Mister Sure: I love that space remark, Happy Imagination. No one could survive there or here without you. Let's keep going.

At that time, Girl From Space was already considering her own startup business ideas, but she was actually embarrassed to share them with Man-Rhythm. Surprisingly for her, the ideas had more to do with ART than Hi-tech.

Girl From Space: Shall I tell Man-Rhythm or not about my great desire to develop my own startup called "Parking For Fun"?

Gray Reality Whispering Around: You already have a job at the Hi-Tech Park in Minsk. Why even bother to have some extra projects on your own?

Anyway, I will absorb all your ideas. I keep all the Hi-tech folks in my big, heavy grip.

Mister Sure: Girl From Space invited some successful young people to her special event. Man-Rhythm was not invited.

Girl From Space: Ladies and gentlemen, I present a startup, named "Parking For Fun", for young businessmen and women. You are all welcome to park all your Hi-tech ideas here, and have fun while doing art, fashion and other CREATIVE projects.

Blue Bag Follow Me: Cuckoo. It was just about the right time for her to get out from under the guardianship of Man-Rhythm!

Mister Sure: Kind of. But not really. Because at the same time, Girl From Space accepted his invitation and she began to learn more about venture capital. She enrolled herself in another Hi-tech adventure back in Moscow. Girl From Space was now serious and focused.

Moscow: O-o-oooh! Now you have changed, and I give you much better options. You are staying in a nice hotel with a shower in the room and a tasty breakfast, and it is right on the corner of your Boutique Venture Event.

Girl From Space: Dear Hi-tech people in Moscow and in other cities on this Earth, we are going to achieve something really BIG.

Happy Imagination:
BIG! That's yummy in
my tummy!

EAGLE FREEDOM

Mister Sure: After Girl From Space got back to Minsk from Moscow, she got a call from Big Guy.

Big Guy: Hi. There is one Mysterious Lecturer who is coming to visit our youth community. She will be teaching about Eagle Freedom. Do you want to come?

Girl From Space: Wait. Did you say "freedom"?

Blue Bag Follow Me: Cuckoo. The image of Blue Paratrooper flashed across her film!

Mister Sure: The same day Girl From Space entered the room dressed very elegantly. She had on a fancy pink dress and bright pink shoes. She noticed that the room had hanging posters with smiling faces of young people.

Mysterious Lecturer: Please have a seat and relax, Girl From Space. My name is Mysterious Lecturer. Today we will have lots of fun. Thank you for coming. I also have one question for you. Who do you think you are?

Happy Imagination: It was very straightforward. I even lost my breath for a second. Then I caught it.

Mister Sure: Girl From Space closed her eyes. The memory of her childhood in the village and Brest, together with her dancing and singing and those revolutionary experiences and the Hi-tech career and some of those incredible Hi-tech adventures, all together, were rolling in her film. There was Man-Rhythm, Blue Paratrooper and that new friend she had recently met, Big Guy. Then Innovative Bulbs appeared there too. She heard a mixed sound of their voices in that film.

Echo: You are in charge of this bright future! Find freedom first! Girl From Space, awake? You are a successful Hi-tech girl!

Girl From Space: I am a hero who is ready to go somewhere far.

Blue Bag Follow Me: Cuckoo.

Mister Sure: Girl From Space opened her eyes.

Mysterious Lecturer: Wow. So good! And now, would you mind trying to negotiate with other people in this room using one sound: 'meow'?

Mister Sure: All the people in the room started meowing at the same time. In a flash, Girl From Space began to feel uncomfortable. She instinctively rejected a meowing girl next to her, even though that girl looked nice.

Girl From Space: This girl next to me is an imposter.

False Girl: What? I am calm and confident. What do you want from me?

Mysterious Lecturer: Girls, stay calm. Now it

is time to play another important game. Who wants to be a leader of two people? And who wants to be a leader of ten?

Girl From Space: I do not like to make commands in order to manage ten people. But I do like the idea of having wings and being able to fly like an eagle. I choose to lead the group of two!

False Girl: I will surely take ten! Stupid Girl From Space.

Happy Imagination: It is just like the beginning of a battle! Is everyone buckled up on the White Holyship? Brilliant Baggie, where are you?

Mister Sure: He is here next to me. Haha.

Mysterious Lecturer: Please leaders, stay calm and focused! Now come toward your people and kneel down with them.

Girl From Space: Do people foresee their future while standing on their knees? I am staring at the group of ten with their leader and an incredibly strong feeling is filling up inside of me.

Brave Heart: No hiccup!

Mister Sure: Space attention! It is going to be a Spacy solo on Earth! Ready?

Brave Heart: I feel unusually strong and powerful, even it feels like my feet are fixed in the concrete floor. I feel like I am waving like a tree during a storm. I also feel the power that is coming from my united being with my partners as my wings. It seems we equal one. Is this the power of the TRINITY?

Mister Sure: This was the kind of another reality that was waiting for Girl From Space.

Happy Imagination: Trinity is a cool thing. I get it.

Gray Reality Whispering Around: Come on. Stop this silly game. Where is this Mysterious Lecturer coming from?

Mister Sure: Well, it was enough for Girl From Space to be sparked. We were all very excited while seeing her making those first steps to find freedom.

Gray Reality Whispering Around: Excuse me, sir, but freedom from what?

SYSTEM OF SYSTEMS

FOLLOW ME

HAPPY IMAGINATION

Mister Sure: Let's meet someone new in the story.

As we already know, Gray Reality Whispering Around tried to defocus Girl From Space from her bright vision of her special mission. But Girl From Space was able to deal with those attacks. Was she? I think she was!

However, there was someone bigger than *Gray Reality Whispering Around*. It was impossible to escape it, even for Girl From Space. Of course, it was not a one-day hunting event. It was a long, long process, but not visible and not even something Girl From Space could feel. Until one day.

Blue Bag Follow Me: Cuckoo. It is like you are a tiny fish that lives in the tummy of a huge, huge fish and you have no idea about it until one day you see that you are actually in the tummy! And there is no way to get out. Phew.

Girl From Space: What is wrong with me?

Happy Imagination: Oopsy. Blue Baggie, keep our special drum close to you. We may need it soon. Mister Sure, what was wrong with Girl From Space?

Mister Sure: Girl From Space was finally unveiling the greatest enemy in the universe: System Of Systems. She began to feel a big wave of weariness throughout her body and soul. And it was destroying her! It was like someone was blocking the flow of her energy and she could not

recover at all. She felt worse and worse.

Then one day System Of Systems started to talk to Girl From Space.

System Of Systems: Welcome to my slavery world, Dear! You are smart and you can now see that there are millions of slaves here in ME. They are all sitting in one big swamp. And that is the other name you can call me. Ha-ha-ha.

Mister Sure: It was a birthday party for Girl From Space. The guests were busy with food and drinks, but Girl From Space was in a never-before-experienced panic that alarmed all that was rolling in her mind-heart film!

Girl From Space: How did I get here? Is it the end? Is there any way for me to get away from System Of Systems?

Blue Bag Follow Me: There was a way for her to be free! There was a team of other space friends to help her out. But a certain action was required from her. At least one word!

Happy Imagination: That is so nice of you, being saved here on the White Spaceship, Blue Boogity-Boo!

Girl From Space: There should be SOMEONE THERE, up, up above this universe. I am Girl From Space and I am caught in the darkest place in the world. Please help me, SOMEONE THERE! It is my entire

human and alien calling for SOS. I want to get out of such a dark world!

Radiant Ray: Hi. I am Radiant Ray. I am also like Blue Paratrooper from Space. She does not know me yet. I am

excited for her.

Tom-tom-tom. Tom-tom-tom... Happy Birthday, Girl From Space!

SOS-REPLY

SKY
SKY
SKY
IDEAS
the Hi-Tech Park in Guangzhou

Mister Sure: A couple of days after her birthday, Girl From Space entered her office with her hair colored an inky black. She dyed her hair to express her deep protest of being inside of System Of Systems. She felt desperate and suffered a lot. Girl From Space was not really up to any tasks from Man-Rhythm. She even lost interest in her job and all Passionate Scientists.

Man-Rhythm: What is up with you, my Dear? Oh, look at the color of your hair. Such a nest for crows!

Girl From Space: Does he not know anything about System Of Systems? He is also a slave, just like me. But he does not see it yet. Poor Man-Rhythm.

Man-Rhythm: Looks like you do not want to talk. Well, I will let you be. I am going to have a call with the Hi-tech world!

Mister Sure: Suddenly, a speedy wind blew her door open. And right there, a group of Chinese Passionate Scientists, headed by Blue Paratrooper, entered the room.

Blue Paratrooper: Ni hao, Girl From Space! How are you doing? You recently pushed the signal SOS, and here I am.

Girl From Space: Wow, this is amazing! Many things have happened since I met you. I am a slave now. All people are slaves here. Do you know this?

Blue Paratrooper: Your slavery is a part of the plan for you to find the freedom. I brought some people from the Hi-Tech Park in Guangzhou with me. Please never stop taking care of Passionate Scientists. Never!

Echo: Take care!

Girl From Space: I will have to find energy to do what Blue Paratrooper asked me.

Hey, Man-Rhythm, let's make a really, really big Hi-tech event in Minsk for Passionate Scientists from Guangzhou. Some of them just got here.

Man-Rhythm: I am so lucky to have you, Girl From Space! Look at me! I feel so good! I am dancing!

Mister Sure: So, Blue Bag Follow Me, what did you see through your space magnifier about what just happened there?

Blue Bag Follow Me: A space event!

Blue Paratrooper came because Girl From Space sent an SOS to the universe. He brought with him a group of Chinese people from the city Guangzhou. He asked her, with now having an inky black color hair and not much energy saved inside of her, to take care of Passionate Scientists across the entire Earth. Girl From Space was inspired and so was Man-Rhythm, even though she knew now that all of them were in System Of Systems. Right, Mister Sure?

IDEA
IDEA IDEA IDEA
IDEA IDEA
IDEA IDEA
I am DANCING
MINSK
GUANGZHOU

SKY

FOLLOW ME

Mister Sure: Let me fix
the crease on that
epaulette, there on your
shoulder!

Happy Imagination:
Imagine that. Blue Baggie
Follow Me just got the
rank of General! Tom!

Mister Sure: Friends, let
the White Spaceship
keep going!

MEOW!

IDEA
IDEA
IDEA
IDEA
IDEA
IDEA
IDEA
IDEA
IDEA
IDEA
IDEA
IDEA
IDEA
Hi-tech
Hi-tech
Hi-tech
Hi-tech
System Of Systems
Haha

Mister Sure: It was a big task for Girl From Space to accomplish. Lots of Passionate Scientists would arrive from Guangzhou to visit and collaborate with Passionate Scientists in Minsk. Everyone would reach out to her and want to know when and how everything was going to happen.

Girl From Space was on the phone, answering many, many questions; she was on her laptop, creating lots and lots of plans for the meetings; she worked with a team of Passionate Hi-tech Designers to build an exhibition; she was a really inspired Hi-tech girl OPERATING in System Of Systems.

Guangzhou: I am so honored, Girl From Space. I will send you the best of my Passionate Scientists. By the way, I am a fast-growing city in southern China. Please, come to visit me one day! I have exotic fruits and blooming trees all year round!

Mister Sure: Everything was going perfect in the preparation, until Guangzhou reached out to Girl From Space again.

Guangzhou: Hi, Girl From Space. My Passionate Scientists are buzzing. Someone told them that it is not really safe for them to travel to your city. They are thinking about the cancellation of their big delegation!

Happy Imagination: Tom-tom-tom-tomity-tom-tom! General Blue Bag, hanging out here on the White Spaceship with your special magnifier, did you even stop to think that maybe those Chinese Passionate Scientists that Blue Paratrooper brought to Minsk discovered something and informed all other Passionate Scientists in Guangzhou?

Blue Bag Follow Me: Nope! It was that OPPORTUNITY for Girl From Space to prove her strength. It was that NARROW gate.

Gray Reality Whispering Around: Ha-ha-ha. Too narrow. Oh yeah.

Mister Sure: Space! Girl From Space had many ideas about building a plan. First, she knocked on the door at the office of Man-Rhythm.

Man-Rhythm: I cannot help you here, Dear. You know that better than I do now. Think of something. But be quick!

Mister Sure: While Girl From Space was sitting at her desk and thinking about her ideas, the image of Blue Paratrooper crossed her film.

Echo: Take care of Passionate Scientists. Follow your heart!

Girl From Space: I do not really know about the whole situation. But I believe that if I do something with all my heart, other people will feel it. I have to be honest and NEGOTIATE. Yes!

Happy Imagination: Meow?

Mister Sure: Haha. Meow-meow-meow! Girl From Space took a deep breath and dialed the phone.

Girl From Space: Dear Guangzhou and all your Passionate Scientists: We are friends. We are not inviting you into danger. We are inviting you to come here to win. Let's conquer our fears together. We are here for all of you. And you are welcome to come here and be for all of us, too. Let's celebrate together. We will win. I have no doubt!

Guangzhou: Stay on the line, Girl From Space. Our main Passionate Scientist, his name is Bu Shuo, is ready to talk to you now.

Bu Shuo: Dear Girl From Space, you are a brave young woman helping us when we seem to be stuck. I want to meet you in person. And I will do it now! I am coming and I am bringing the big

delegation of all Passionate Scientists! See you soon!

Mister Sure: Girl From Space dropped to her knees in her office and started to cry. The big Hi-tech event was a great success for her, even though it was all happening in System Of Systems.

After the event, Girl From Space became even more tired than before. She thought that she fulfilled the task Blue

Paratrooper gave her. But she still had other things to deal with.

Blue Bag Follow Me: The main thing? That it was all POSSIBLE for her, even when she was still inside System Of Systems!

Happy Imagination: Because the rest of us were on the Holy White Spaceship!

98

COME ON!

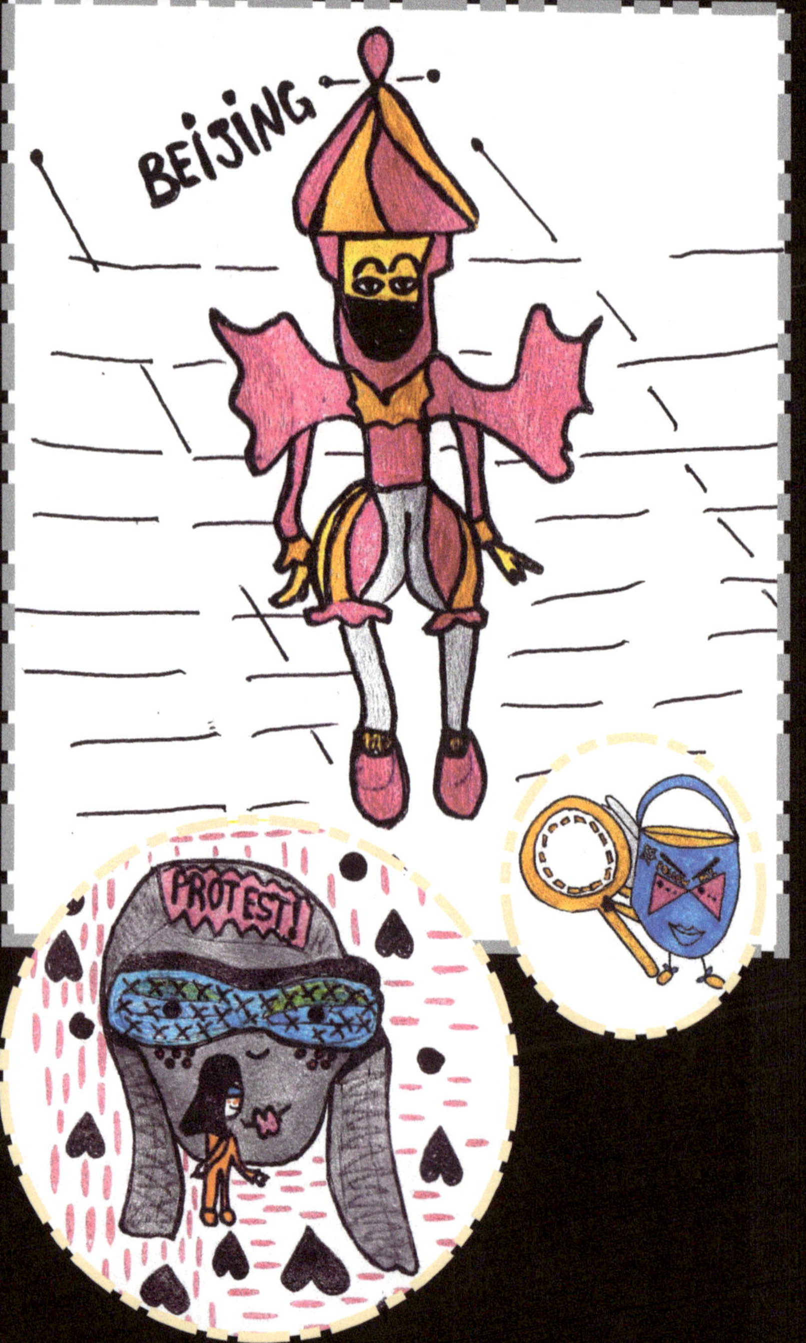
BEIJING
PROTEST!

Mister Sure: It was autumn.

Happy and excited after the big Hi-tech event, Man-Rhythm was ready to prepare Girl From Space for another Hi-tech adventure, which was all the way in Beijing, the capital of China. This time Girl From Space was not joyful. All that she could think about was how to get out of System Of Systems.

Beijing: Well, well, well. Just do it and come to me. For sure, it will be a different experience for you here than Shanghai. My weather in September is very hot. And I prepared for you a very, very busy, one-month stay. Are you ready for that? I also heard about your success with the Guangzhou city in Minsk. Aren't you a little bit tired?

Blue Bag Follow Me: Detection, Mister Sure. Girl From Space took a plane and stepped out onto the land of Beijing!

Girl From Space: It is really hot here. And I hate my inky black hair color.

Beijing: You made it, Girl From Space. The hotel I have for you is nice. But you cannot open any windows to get some fresh air if you need it. There is NO fresh air in ME!

Mister Sure: The whole month Girl From Space felt miserable and not comfortable at all in Beijing. She was barely paying attention to other Passionate Scientists, even though Blue Paratrooper asked her to take care of them. They all came to Beijing from different cities. Passionate Scientists had heard so many good things about her, and they were really disappointed.

Blue Bag Follow Me:
There was no action or any drive from Girl From Space anymore. And that was not a bad thing! That was a normal stage for her to go through.

Happy Imagination:
How easy it is to say. But how hard it was for her, Blue Boopity-Boo General.

Mister Sure: So true.

Finally, Girl From Space returned to Minsk from Beijing. The weather was cold and gloomy. A good contrast for her. She had just put down her suitcases after the trip when her boyfriend told her that he was going to have a big celebration of his birthday with lots of friends that night. Girl From Space quickly dressed and they arrived at the restaurant just in time.

Girl From Space: Oh wow, there are lots of food and drinks on the table. Lots of friends walking around. But I feel so tired.

No one really cares about anything here in System Of Systems. EVERYONE, including my boyfriend, is playing a role and covering their true face with a mask. Who knows what all these imposters are really thinking about. Seems like nothing really deep... Where is Blue Paratrooper? How can I get out of this swamp?

FOLLOW ME
HAPPY IMAGINATION

Boyfriend: Hey, my love. Do you want to give me a toast? Today is actually my birthday!

Mister Sure: Girl From Space stood up and after she looked at every single MASK sitting at the table, she turned toward her boyfriend.

Girl From Space: I love you. You are the best for me. Happy Birthday.

Mister Sure: Girl From Space closed her eyes and took one of those deep breaths.

Girl From Space: I just now lied to every single person here. Can they even feel anything in this swamp?

Gray Reality Whispering Around: Just say... I gave up on my special mission. SAY IT! It is really so easy. You can say it now: I gave up on my special mission.

Blue Bag Follow Me: Hey, Gray Reality! Get-get-get out of her way! It is not over yet. Not even close.

Girl From Space: It is over for me. It is over... I do not have any energy left. I feel as if I am sinking like a crashed alien deep into the dark swamp: System Of Systems.

Happy Imagination: Hey Baggie, we desperately need our space lifebuoy called Push! Go find it and bring it, quick-quick-quick!

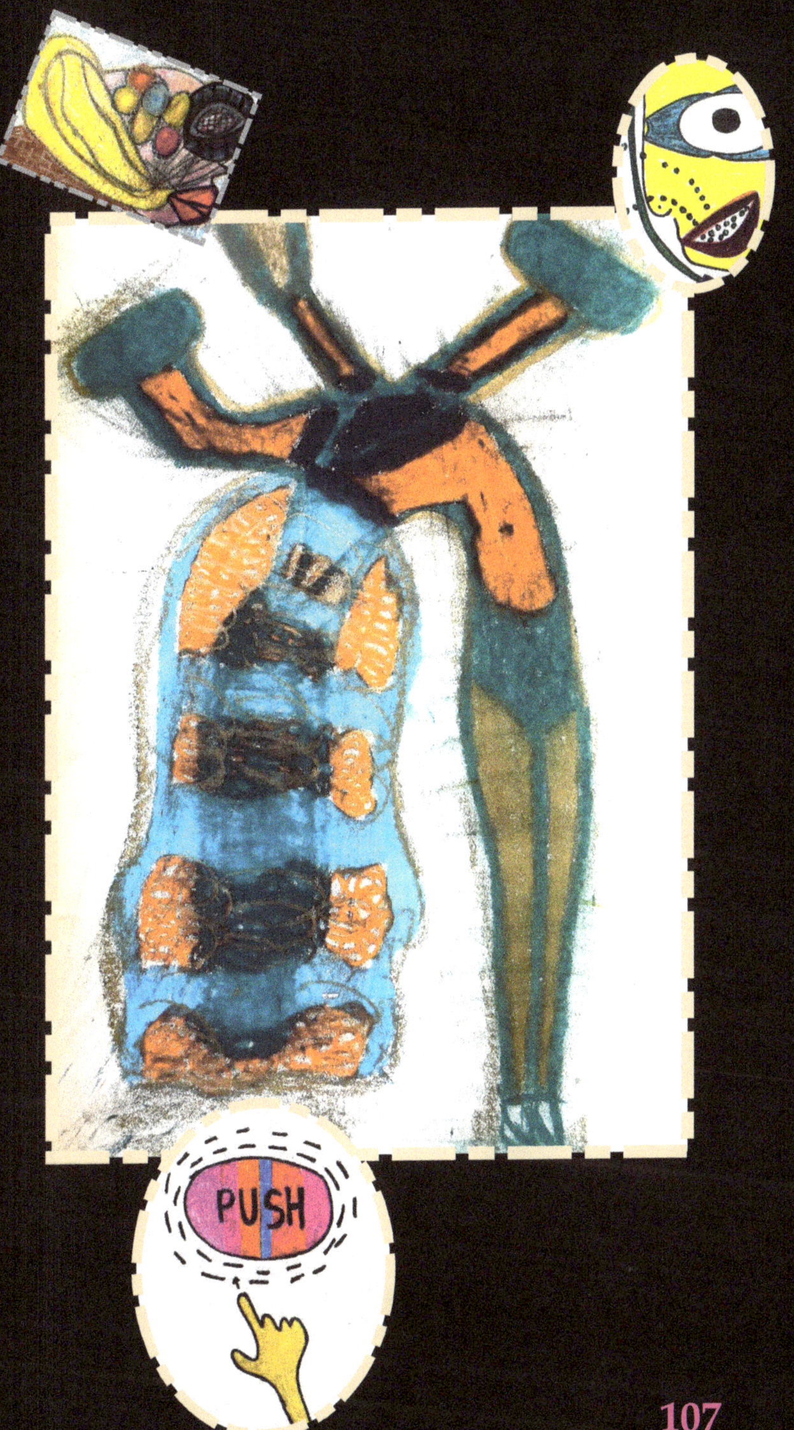

PUSH

CONTAINER

Hohoho
BELARUS
LIGHT
HEAVY
PAST

Mister Sure: It was winter.

Girl From Space entered into her office with a sad face. It was gloomy and cold outside. Then suddenly, she noticed a happy face with a smile sitting in her chair.

Belarus: Ho ho ho. I am here to help you. I did not forget you with your brave heart, how you marched and shouted that powerful slogan about freedom for me on the streets of Minsk ten years ago. So here. The movie on this DVD that I am holding in my hand is for you. Please watch it as soon as you can.

Holy-Space-Holy! Who could even think about that kind of r-e-v-o-l-u-t-i-o-n?

ME! Silly Happy Hippie Maggie. Our space magnifier shows that Belarus was helping the White Spaceship. Got it?

Mister Sure: Ho ho ho. Girl From Space grabbed the DVD and drove back to her home, the apartment where she lived with her boyfriend (who she really didn't love, like she said she did). She parked the car and ran-ran-ran toward the apartment building and then upstairs to the fifth floor. There was no time for using the elevator!

Girl From Space's breathing was rushing and the movement of her chest gave it away. She opened the door of her apartment, holding in her hands her laptop and the DVD. She did not take her shoes off, she simply walked into the living room. She sat down on the carpet on the floor by the coffee table. She opened the DVD and slipped it into her laptop. And there she sat, on the floor, holding her laptop on her knees, watching her full-length film. In an INSTANT, it was all happening to her.

So, what was there in that single film that made Girl From Space able to make an effort to get away from System Of Systems? It was about a container! The container with a label that said: PAST. It was the new way Girl From Space began to see System Of Systems: in the past.

Blue Bag Follow Me:
Girl From Space wanted to be washed from System Of Systems. As if it never happened to her!

Mister Sure: Space is confirming - you got it again. Girl From Space stood up from the floor and placed her laptop on the coffee table. She went to the kitchen and opened some cabinets, she was looking for something. Finally, she found the empty grocery bags and walked from the kitchen, straight to her closet. She quickly started packing some of her clothes into the grocery bags. She added her boots and some jewelry. She was gathering her belongings, rushing around and not really caring about any of them. She felt she needed to be fast! Like having to catch a train that was leaving from the station and she was late.

Suddenly, her phone rang.

Big Guy: Hi there. What are you doing?

Girl From Space: I am taking a RISK!

COLD WINTER

SPORTS CAR

Mister Sure: Girl From Space drove her sports car packed with all her belongings through the snowy streets of Minsk.

She was not happy, but she was not really sad either. She felt empty inside, AGAIN.

Girl From Space: Where should I go now?

Blue Bag Follow Me: What were the options? Time to brainstorm on the White Spaceship!

Happy Imagination: Silly, there should be a place that was especially for her. Like her own p-a-r-a-d-i-s-e.

Mister Sure: Haha. Remember? Miracles are my hobby. You gotta believe.

Girl From Space got a call. It was her friend in System Of Systems. Well, kind of a friend.

Freelance Artist: I want to help, Girl From Space. But I am a weak person, a simple slave. All I can do is find a new apartment for you and pay the rent. Yes, I will pay for it.

Mister Sure: It was snowy and windy. Girl From Space could see white fields of snow through the windows of her new apartment. It was on the outskirts of Minsk and that was okay with her. She had no furniture in the apartment. But it was warm. All that she had were those grocery bags with her belongings that were standing, lonely, on the floor.

Blue Bag Follow Me: She needed at least a bed!

Mister Sure: She got another call from another friend.

Friend-Businessman: I am downstairs. I brought you a bed.

Happy Imagination: Much better. But still. That was not even close to what we have here on our White Spaceship. I hope Girl From Space can have happy dreams! Those are my favorite.

Mister Sure: Girl From Space took a shower and changed. She lay down on the bed and closed her eyes. Then she stood up and went to the bathroom to look at herself in the mirror.

Girl From Space: What shall I do next? Maybe I should do some dancing. Yeah.

Mister Sure: She shook herself like she had some dust on her, and then she put on her jacket and shoes and went downstairs and into her sports car.

118

BATHROOM
DUST
DUST
DUST
DUST

BED

WILLPOWER

Mister Sure: Girl From Space stopped by a dancing supply store and bought herself a tight ballet outfit. Then she drove to a ballet school, located in downtown Minsk.

When Girl From Space opened the door to a not-so-spacious room where she faced a lot of mirrors, it was challenging for her to see her image in those mirrors. Were they not welcoming her? She felt vulnerable as never before. However, there were nice girls rehearsing some movements in two lines in that room. They greeted Girl From Space with their happy smiles.

Nice Girls: The teacher is almost here. Stand and rehearse with us in any line you like.

Mister Sure: Girl From Space stood in the second line behind one of those nice girls. She was trying to hide, but she could not. She saw her entire image wherever she turned. And then she heard a loud voice.

Ballet Teacher: Look at this! A new grasshopper is in our class. Hello.

Mister Sure: Ballet Teacher came toward Girl From Space and slowly walked around her inspecting every part of her body.

Ballet Teacher: Your back looks horrible. How did you find us, grasshopper?

Ballet? I am thinking here. Was it a way for her

to tighten herself with some discipline? Looking inside for a different view?

Our space magnifier shows that Ballet Teacher was really hard on Girl From Space. The harder, the better result!

Mister Sure: Girl From Space felt like a soft ball to be kicked in her life-film. That was why she became an open, comfortable target for Ballet Teacher's critique. Feeling that hardness of circumstances around her, Girl From Space could barely move her feet while facing a strict and, maybe, unfair attitude toward her from Ballet Teacher. But she came to the next class, and then she showed up in the one after that. It was not even in Girl From Space's mind to quit. She worked hard every time she was there. And she learned to dance and move, PASSING all the not-so-pleasant-attention-getting comments from Ballet Teacher.

Ballet Teacher: Look at you. I thought you were a grasshopper. But now I see in you WILLPOWER. Impressed, impressed!

Mister Sure: Girl From Space was not new to this word - willpower. We all know that. But now she was preparing herself in her mind and heart for another big step. She was determined to do it, no matter what.

Happy Imagination: It was a tight space, am I right? I can see it in my m-i-n-d.

HAPPY IMAGINATION
FOLLOW ME

ENTRANCE-MAP

STRETCH
YOURSELF
JUMP!

Mister Sure: It was February when one morning Girl From Space woke up and realized that she had been living in her empty apartment for exactly two months. What was she looking at while lying in her bed? She was looking at the light-colored wallpaper all around on the walls, then through her window, watching the lonely morning snowstorm.

Girl From Space stood up from her bed and went to her bathroom to look at her image in the mirror. By the way, her hair was golden again. That was a big deal.

Girl From Space: I cannot wait any longer. I AM READY.

Blue Bag Follow Me: Cuckoo. It was time to prepare to go through her next narrow gate, another opportunity!

Happy Imagination: The narrower, the better the opportunity, my Blue General. Envision the eye of a needle and then through the needle eye - a big happy elephant with his WELCOME sign.

Mister Sure: Haha. Girl From Space took a shower, got dressed, and was soon on her way to the office at the Hi-Tech Park in Minsk. When she arrived, she went straight to Man-Rhythm's office and knocked on his door.

Man-Rhythm: Who is there? I am on a call with the Hi-tech world! I will be with you shortly.

 It's me. No problem.

golden hair color! Congrats! Haha.

Mister Sure: Girl From Space decided to wait in her office. She sat down on her chair and opened her laptop. Then she got an idea to look at some pictures on her laptop from last year's events that she organized in Minsk. While doing that, her face lit up and her eyes opened wide and she smiled so softly when she found the pictures from her startup, Parking For Fun. The smile vanished as quickly as it came. Right then Man-Rhythm entered the room.

Blue Bag Follow Me: Cuckoo. He was always there at the right time.

Man-Rhythm: Wow, you are back to your normal

Mister Sure: Girl From Space did not say anything back to Man-Rhythm. Then Man-Rhythm stopped laughing and paused. It was a deep moment for her film. They were looking into each other's eyes. And it seemed like it was a long, quiet moment of HOPE in System Of Systems. That hope was so true and so pure that it somehow connected their hearts.

During that long moment of hope, Man-Rhythm seemed to understand Girl From Space as never before. Then he whispered, like he was afraid that someone else could hear him.

Man-Rhythm: What's the matter, my Dear?

SPACE DESERT
GATE

CHANGCHUN
SPACE DESERT
MAP
HO
PE

Mister Sure: Man-Rhythm looked around and then came closer to her. Girl From Space felt only then, the very moment of their true partnership.

Girl From Space: I am asking you for help and collaboration. Maybe this step that I want to make is not only for me, but for all of us. I feel it that way. I want to leave HERE. I must leave. I have to go somewhere far, really far away. And I also have a name for that place. It is called SPACE DESERT.

Mister Sure: Girl From Space stood up from her chair and went to the map on the wall. The map had some marks about locations of where all Passionate Scientists were on the Earth.

Girl From Space: Let's take a look where we have the farthest located Passionate Scientists. Let's announce to them that we are going to open an ENTERPRISE there, and I am going to be there to help.

Mister Sure: While Man-Rhythm's eyes were following Girl From Space, he touched his chin with one of his hands and, holding it like that, he came toward the map.

Man-Rhythm: The farthest we have is in Changchun, all the way in northern China. Wait a minute, now. I actually like this idea. I have always had a dream to open an enterprise somewhere really far away from my home.

133

Mister Sure: Man-Rhythm now looked excited. It was a new direction, new gate for him that he had never seen as a possibility before. Realizing that, he rejoiced and looked at Girl From Space.

Man-Rhythm: I believe in you, Girl From Space.

Mister Sure: Then Man-Rhythm announced a fair idea that crossed his mind.

Man-Rhythm: You know what, I will go with you. Yes, definitely. I will go. And I will take a couple of Passionate Scientists with us. I want to help you to settle in and then I will come back to Minsk. Someone needs to be here too. Sound like a plan?

Mister Sure: It was decided that Changchun was Space Desert.

Happy Imagination: How smart that Man-Rhythm suggested to help Girl From Space and go with her, at least for a little bit. N-i-c-e guy.

Brave Heart: Hope so.

Blue Bag Follow Me: Girl From Space would go to Changchun to open an enterprise there. It was another step out of her past, System Of Systems, and right into Space Desert! Right, Mister Sure?

Mister Sure: Yes, Space General!

Blue Bag Follow Me:
Mister Sure, may I have one more snack-in-a-tube?

PRIEST-ANGELS

HAPPY IMAGINATION

Mister Sure: There were only two weeks left for Girl From Space in Minsk. What should she take with her on that new, big, important, and soon-to-happen mission?

That night Girl From Space was not in a rush to go to her empty apartment. She did not want to go to her ballet class, either. She parked her sports car in the snowy neighborhood of her empty apartment and decided to get out and walk around. It was a new district that she actually did not know anything about.

While she was walking, she passed a big, dark, snowy park. Then she noticed lights on in a tiny building in the deepest part of the dark park. The snowflakes were falling from the sky, dancing and inviting her to check it out. First, the sound of flying crows and tall snowy trees in the park did not seem welcoming to her at all. However, Girl From Space stepped in and kept walking on a forgotten snowy path into another little world. She also felt cold on her toes. It was a really frosty night.

When Girl From Space came close to the building, she opened the door and saw two Priest-Angels preparing for a service inside. She felt comfortable to walk right in, even though they did not say anything to her. She quietly took a seat on a back bench and kept looking at Priest-Angels and inspecting her surroundings: wood walls with a few drawings of holy people on them and different statues on the altar. Then she switched her attention back to Priest-

Angels. They were wearing long coats.

While observing them, Girl From Space noticed that one of them looked friendlier to her than the other. She could see the special light in his EYES. Girl From Space also felt peaceful there. Maybe even kind of relaxed. It was like a little capsule inside System Of Systems, the neutral and free one! Finally, some other people quietly started to show up. There were about eight of them by the time the service began.

Blue Bag Follow Me: Mister Sure, can I describe the service with the help of our space magnifier?

Mister Sure: Please do.

Blue Bag Follow Me: He-he-he. Our space magnifier shows that Priest-Angels were holding a chain with a cup on the end that was making a cloud! They were swinging that chain, so that the cup and the cloud were swinging too, creating an interesting geometrical abstract image of scales!

The SCALES OF LIFE - the image of choice.

As they were greeting the people who had come, the warm air, like a pure white flow, was streaming from their mouths. They were two special ANGELS in that tiny cold building in the big, dark, snowy park!

Then they had a preaching part. It was about the Father and the Son and the angels in heaven. Their preaching sound was like a rhyme.

Sound of a song? Just like they were not just saying it; they were singing it.

Girl From Space: How fun! I feel like I want to come here again.

Happy Imagination: Yippeee and tiddily-diddily-do!

Mister Sure: Girl From Space showed up in that building EVERY night! She chose a seat closer and closer each time. But never really took the ones in the first row. Priest-Angels always performed the same routine there during the services. Girl From Space was always quiet and still.

Day by day passed, and soon the two weeks were coming to an end. Girl From Space seemed to be peaceful and not in any kind of panic. But let's see.

Girl From Space bought a suitcase at the supermarket and packed all her belongings from the grocery bags. Actually, there was something missing in her suitcase. She did not put her jewelry in there. Nothing at all. She gave it away just the other day. Some to her mom and some to her sister and some to her friends.

Where was I? Okay. So that last night when her suitcase was packed, she dressed warm and put her belongings in her sports car and then decided to drive to the tiny building in the dark park for the last time before her departure to Changchun. It was a surprise for her when after the service the friendlier looking Priest-Angel simply came toward her and sat quietly beside her on the cold wooden bench.

Priest-Angel: How is everything with you?

Blue Bag Follow Me: Cuckoo. Girl From Space was about to answer that question.

Girl From Space: Am I supposed to confess my sins? I have never done this before.

Mister Sure: Girl From Space stopped for a moment. What was she actually up to? What did she want to share with Priest-Angel? What kind of sins did she have? Is it the sin that she left her boyfriend? OR did not invite Man-Rhythm on her special presentation, "Parking For Fun"? OR the sin that she hated System Of Systems? OR maybe the one that she was disappointed in those professors in her college? OR maybe this one: Little Girl From Space sometimes did scare those farm animals in the village of her grandparents. She was simply chasing them while singing a song that she made up with your help, Happy Imagination.

Happy Imagination:
Oopsy. Oh dear ME.

Blue Bag Follow Me: I also see, Mister Sure, through our space magnifier, that there were many other little issues. But not much, only

normal stuff. She and her sister never played together, so sometimes they had arguments and were running and hiding behind their mom in order not to be hair-pulled by the other.

And one day Girl From Space took a 100-ruble banknote that she found under the mattress of her parents. There were many banknotes under that mattress. She took just one. But later, one night her parents awakened her and asked if she took one. She said no. And then she felt bad and could not fall back to sleep.

Happy Imagination:
Holy Space. That was like a nonstop roller coaster! Phew. Ready again whenever you are.

Mister Sure: Meanwhile, Priest-Angel kept looking at her with patience and a sense of calm, and maybe even a kind of love from the Father in Heaven that was dwelling within him. Realizing that his ATTENTION toward her was like nothing she had ever felt from anybody ever in her life, Girl From Space all of sudden began to cry. She was trying to hold back her heavy rolling tears on her face, but she could not control any of them. They kept falling right into her film.

Finally, Girl From Space let every tear spill freely from her eyes. It took many minutes and then she was ready to continue the conversation with Priest-Angel, who was patiently waiting for her to speak again.

Girl From Space: I am flying tonight to Space

Desert. All that I have is FAITH in my special mission to find freedom that Blue Paratrooper told me about.

Mister Sure: Girl From Space took that deep breath again. Perhaps she was processing her own just-said words. But she had no doubt that Priest-Angel was not confused hearing those words at all. She did not even question in her mind if he actually knew System Of Systems and Gray Reality Whispering Around and maybe other black realities that were ahead of her on her way to that freedom.

Priest-Angel was still in his entire image – the body, hands, even eyelashes – did not move at all while listening and looking at Girl From Space – the movements of her lips, switching emotions on her face, her shine-with-hope eyes that were still a little bit wet after the crying she had a few minutes before. Then Priest-Angel, without changing his calm demeanor, concluded. It seemed that only his eyes were talking, carrying that deep compassion for Girl From Space.

Priest-Angel: All that I can do is pray for you. I also have a tiny book filled with one simple prayer for you. Take it with you.

Mister Sure: Priest-Angel finally moved. He took the tiny book out of his pocket and handed it to Girl From Space.

Priest-Angel: It is time.

Mister Sure: While Girl From Space kept looking at Priest-Angel she started walking toward the door, holding the tiny book tightly with both her hands.

Girl From Space: Good bye! I will mail you a card from Space Desert! I will let you know how it will be for me there!

Mister Sure: Priest-Angel did not say any words about that. But he kept looking at her.

Happy Imagination: Mister General, oopsy, Mister Sure, I think the Trinity that Brave Heart experienced during those games led by Mysterious Lecturer was dwelling in that small frozen building in the dark, cold, snowy park, too. I mean at that particular time frame, of course.

Holy-Spaceship-Holy. Our White Spaceship is about to make that big pit stop called Space Dessert. Oopsy. I mean Desert!

Blue Bag Follow Me: Tom! Tom!

146

BEFORE DEPARTURE

GATE
SPACE DESERT

MY
LORD!

Mister Sure: Girl From Space left the tiny building and then the dark park. She walked back to her sports car and then drove back to her apartment.

It was a very cold night. Her hands were cold and almost frozen. And it seemed that all of her body was shaking. But it was not only because the cold air inside of that tiny building affected her, or that outside the windy, snowy weather did not spare her, or even because she was leaving her hometown of Minsk. It was a desperate shake, deep to the bone, before the great unknown that she was about to step into, all by herself.

When Girl From Space parked her car by her apartment, she noticed her friends, Freelance Artist and Friend-Businessman, and another person. The three of them were waiting for her by the entrance to the empty apartment, which was an uncomfortable feeling of cold, while letting Girl From Space go into another world! Freelance Artist looked at Girl From Space with hope in his eyes and took the key for the apartment. Friend-Businessman took back the bed and hugged her instead. Girl From Space put the tiny prayer book Priest-Angel gave to her in her suitcase and she was soon dropped off at the airport by that third person. That friend also promised to take care of her BMW.

Now Girl From Space was standing at the airport in Minsk. She was waiting for Man-Rhythm and two other Passionate Scientists to arrive.

While waiting, she tried

to take that deep breath, but she was interrupted when she saw one Passionate Scientist that she knew.

Passionate Scientist was ten feet away from her, sitting in a chair that had a lot of cushions and he kept smacking them for no particular reason. He was talking and laughing with other Passionate Scientists that were sitting around him in those comfortable chairs.

In that moment Passionate Scientist noticed Girl From Space, too. Her heart began to beat faster.

Passionate Scientist: Hey Girl From Space! I cannot believe my eyes! How are you, Dear?

Blue Bag Follow Me: Cuckoo. It was one of those Passionate Scientists from her Shanghai Hi-tech adventure who had to buy silk for his wife!

Happy Imagination: We are approaching Exodus here. Hold on tightly to your seat, General Blue Bag Follow Me. If you close your eyes, it might even be more fun! Wheeeeee!

Mister Sure: That was the thing. Girl From Space's eyes lit up when she saw Passionate Scientist stand up and come toward her. And then he hugged her like she was his best friend and started sharing all those amazing memories about their Hi-tech adventure in Shanghai, which actually happened three years ago! Finally, after his long discourse, and Girl From

Space saying next to nothing, Passionate Scientist asked her one very simple question.

Passionate Scientist: But where are you going now?

WHITE SPACESHIP

Blue Bag Follow Me:
I wonder... if Girl From Space had known Space Desert ahead of time, would she have skipped the adventure? There will be more FAITH in Space Desert to COLLECT into my pockets!

Happy Imagination:
I think we s-o-l-d out, if you can imagine that.

Mister Sure: Ooh, Girl From Space will not have an easy time in Space Desert. There she will deal with old and new enemies - the whole band of them will come from all around. The good news? Her new space friends will come for her in Space Desert, too.

Thank you, dear friend. Please consider staying connected. Stay charged.

To be Continued.

Happy Imagination:
Hola! Oopsy. I mean adious!

BRAVE HEART

CHEWITS
American
Tourists

MAP
CHANGCHUN
SPACE DESERT
HOPE

PUSH

www.ingramcontent.com/pod-product-compliance
Lightning Source LLC
Chambersburg PA
CBHW051114300726
48981CB00002B/126